Uh-oh, Cleo

Cleo

Jessica Harper

ILLUSTRATED BY
Jon Berkeley

G. P. Putnam's Sons

G. P. PUTNAM'S SONS
A division of Penguin Young Readers Group.
Published by The Penguin Group.
Penguin Group (USA) Inc., 375 Hudson Street, New York, NY 10014, U.S.A. Penguin Group
(Canada), 90 Eglinton Avenue East, Suite 700, Toronto, Ontario M4P 2Y3, Canada
(a division of Pearson Penguin Canada Inc.). Penguin Books Ltd, 80 Strand, London WC2R
0RL, England. Penguin Ireland, 25 St. Stephen's Green, Dublin 2, Ireland (a division of
Penguin Books Ltd.). Penguin Group (Australia), 250 Camberwell Road, Camberwell,
Victoria 3124, Australia (a division of Pearson Australia Group Pty Ltd). Penguin Books
India Pvt Ltd, 11 Community Centre, Panchsheel Park, New Delhi - 110 017, India. Penguin
Group (NZ), 67 Apollo Drive, Rosedale, North Shore 0745, Auckland, New Zealand (a
division of Pearson New Zealand Ltd.). Penguin Books (South Africa) (Pty) Ltd, 24 Sturdee
Avenue, Rosebank, Johannesburg 2196, South Africa. Penguin Books Ltd, Registered Offices:
80 Strand, London WC2R 0RL, England.

Design by Richard Amari. Text set in Eco 101.

Library of Congress Cataloging-in-Publication Data
Harper, Jessica. Uh-oh, Cleo / Jessica Harper ; illustrated by Jon Berkeley.
p. cm. Summary: What starts out as a perfectly ordinary day in the Small house turns into
Stitches Saturday when Cleo gets a cut on the head after her twin brother, Jack,
accidentally pulls down their "Toy House." [1. Wounds and injuries—Fiction. 2. Sutures—
Fiction. 3. Medical care—Fiction. 4. Brothers and sisters—Fiction. 5. Twins—Fiction.
6. Family life—Illinois—Fiction. 7. Winnetka (Ill.)—Fiction.] I. Berkeley, Jon, ill. II. Title.
PZ7.H231343Uh 2008   [E—dc22 2007027507   ISBN 978-0-399-24671-5

3 5 7 9 10 8 6 4

Chapter 1

I used to wake up most days and think, Okay, good morning, it's another big old regular day. I didn't expect anything special, just the normal: normal this, normal that.

But ever since Stitches Saturday, I wake up not so sure.

Stitches Saturday was a couple of weeks ago, and it started out normal enough. The Little Three (Lily and the baby twins, Ray

and Quinn) were awake first like always. They were eating breakfast by the time the Big Three (me and my twin brother, Jack, and Jenna) showed up in the kitchen.

Ray and Quinn were in their high chairs with baby oatmeal. Lily ate Kix at the table and sang herself a little song.

"Eat your food, don't be rude,
Pepper in the daytime, sugar in the night..."

I think those were the words. You couldn't quite hear because Mrs. Davis (the lady who helps Mom on Saturdays) had the vacuum cleaner going full blast in the hall. Also,

Quinn was banging on his tray, going, "YAH, YAH, YAH, YAH!" Ray rubbed oatmeal between his hands, concentrating, like a scientist making a discovery.

Mom was at the stove making regular grown-up oatmeal for the Big Three. Her apron was tied in a messy bow at the back that wiggled while she stirred. She also sang a song, which you also couldn't quite hear.

I ate my oatmeal fast because the vacuum cleaner and the YAH, YAHs on top of two people singing was pretty annoying. Plus, I wanted to get to the Toy House.

Dad built the Toy House for me and Jack a few Christmases ago. It wasn't really a house, just a bunch of shelves with a pointy piece of wood across the top that looked like a roof. It was all painted red with "Toy House" written on the roof in fancy white letters. It looked beautiful on Christmas morning, all red, white and shiny.

"It looks like a giant piece of candy," Jack said.

"This is where your toys will live," Dad said when I untied the big bow he'd put around it to make it look like a giant present.

Now the Toy House is pretty messy and tired. It's in the room I share with Jack and it's all full of our yo-yos and jacks and dolls and everything. Sometimes in my mind I hear it groaning from all the stuff it has to hold all the time: "Uhhhhh . . ." it'll say when I put the crayon pot back. "Ahhhhh . . ." it'll say when I take the heavy doll box off the second shelf.

Most Saturdays, Jack sets up his soldiers and starts making little wars all over the floor ("Puh-KOW, puh-KOW!") while I get down my doll box and pull out my three favorites. The doll Dad got me in Appalachia is one. She's carved from a single piece of wood and has a stiff blue apron and a face like a strict teacher.

Then there's the Russian doll. She's fancier: she has a flowery dress and a hat like an upside-down cereal bowl. I call her Rapunzel the Russian.

But my most favorite is Anne. She's the doll version of a real-life queen who got her head chopped off by a bad king. This doll's the fanciest, of course, and the most beautiful, because she's a queen. She has this blue silk dress with fur trim around the top, which looks like it might be itchy.

I feel sorry for her because she's headed for a sad end (oh, I shouldn't say *headed*, should I). "We need to take care of her," I told Rapunzel and the Appalachian. I showed them how to give her tea and read to her and everything. "Her life is going to be short, so we have to make sure it's happy."

Me and Jack usually move on to Candy Land when we get tired of the dolls and soldiers. Jenna says it's a game for babies, but we don't care. We LOVE Candy Land.

We push the pieces around the board, landing on candy canes and gumdrops and chocolate kisses until we can't stand it anymore. Jack yells, "Candy craving!" and we run downstairs and out the door. "Chaaarrrge!" We jump on our bikes and ride fast, up the block to Charles Variety. That's the best store in Winnetka for candy. They also sell stuff like batteries and plastic flowers, but who cares.

I get lemon drops and Red Hots and Jack likes Mars bars. We eat it all before we bike home so Mom won't know about it. She says sugar makes us nutty, not to mention rots our teeth.

Also in the Toy House is a cooking pot full of crayons that weighs about a ton.

Mom usually buys us a fresh box of crayons when school starts in the fall. I love the way they look that first day, all lined up in rainbow order: Winter White to Brink Pink to Vivid Violet, and on and on.

My favorite color is Wild Blue Yonder. That usually gets shorter first because I use it for skies, which are big. Colors like Neon Carrot, Asparagus and Eggplant last a long time. We don't like them much; they're too vegetably.

But after a couple of months, all the crayons start to get peely and short and even

Jenna stops putting them in order. Then they get left on the floor and squished and broken. Finally Mom just tosses them all in the pot with last year's crayons, so it can take half an hour to find the Mango Tango or whatever.

Anyway, on Stitches Saturday, I think it was the crayon pot that did it.

Chapter 2

What happened was, after breakfast, me and Jack were playing dolls and soldiers, normal as can be. Then Jenna came barging in. (She never knocks or asks if she can come in, she just barges.)

She got down our tub of plastic animals. ("Ahhhhh," said the Toy House.)

Since her birthday in March, Jenna's been saying she's too grown-up to play now.

12

(Excuse me, she's only ten, okay? And we're eight!) So when she looks like she's playing, she says she's really not, she's "sorting." I don't know why she has to "sort" our toys instead of hers. She has her own Toy House in her room, and it's loaded.

She dumped the animals on the floor and started putting them in groups: lions here, bears there. Then she put them in lines: lion, bear bear, tiger tiger tiger, giraffe giraffe giraffe giraffe. Finally, she had them in a big, neat triangle.

When Jenna got to the elephant row, she started to bump into my dolls, who were trying to have tea.

"Could you puh-LEEZE move?" she said, like it's HER room and HER toys, not mine.

The Appalachian said, "Oooo, bossy, bossy, BOSSY!"

Me and the dolls talk to each other through our minds, not out loud. This comes in handy 'cause we can say whatever we want and not get in trouble.

"Yep, she's a Bossy Cow," Rapunzel the Russian agreed. "Moooo!"

What Jenna didn't notice, but I did, was that Jack was VERY quietly turning his soldiers in her direction, slowly, one by one.

"Oh, okay, Jen, no problem." I scooted

my dolls out of the way; I knew what was coming.

"CHARGE! Puh-KOW! Puh-KOW!" It was war.

"GOOD-BYE, MR. BEAR!" With the soldier in his hand, Jack whacked the bears across the room. "You're HISTORY, MR. LION! Puhh-KOW!" (Lions flyin'.) "YOU SHOULDA STAYED AT THE ZOO, MR. ELEPHANT, puh-KOW!"

The animal war was over really fast. Guess who won.

Jenna jumped up and stamped her foot, squishing a blue camel. "JACK, YOU ARE

16

THE BIGGEST DORK IN THE ENTIRE UNIVERSE!" she yelled, and barged out down the hall.

Jack did the cannibal dance, like he always does when he's made Jenna barge out.

"WE *are the* CANnibals, *bump, bump,*
WE *are the* CANnibals, *bump, bump* . . ."

I got up and did it with him. (You bump your butts together on the *bump bump* part.) But I felt a tiny bit sorry for Jenna. Jack never did stuff like that to me, just her.

"Do YOU know what TIME it is?" Jack

asked me. He sounded like a TV announcer.

"No, what time is it?" I actually did know. He always asked this when it was time for Candy Land.

"DO YOU KNOW what TIME IT IS?" Jack asked me louder.

"Yes."

"You're supposed to say NO," Jack reminded me.

"Okay, okay, NO." I just wanted to get to the game already.

"It's time for . . . *duh, duh, duh DUH, duh DUH* . . ." Jack blew a pretend trumpet. "CANDY LAND!"

It was hard to reach, on the top shelf. But Jack was 1) naughty, and 2) he couldn't wait for Mom to help. He decided to Spider-Man up the Toy House and get the game himself. He started climbing: right foot on the first shelf, hands on the third, uuuuuuupp. Left foot on the second shelf, hands on the roof, uuuuuppp.

The Toy House wiggled and got tippy. "Whoa!" Jack held on tight.

"Uhhhhh . . ." the Toy House groaned.

Then toys started to fall.

First it was just the little stuff, the china fairy and the harmonica.

"Yikes!" Jack stepped down a shelf.

Then came the big stuff: Monopoly and the plastic fruit.

"UHHHHH . . ." The Toy House leaned forward.

Candy Land fell, then checkers, then *Harry Potter* (the first one).

"UHHHHH . . ."

I jumped up.

Tiiiiiiiiiippp . . . my fingernail painting kit, three Lemony Snicket books, Barbie's pink bed . . .

Jack jumped down.

We put up our hands to try and stop it, but the Toy House kept tipping and the big stuff kept coming, faster and faster:

HARRY POTTER (the second one),

JUMP ROPE, MY TEA SET!

**FOUR BARBIE DOLLS
AND ONE KEN!**

A BIG FAT DICTIONARY,

**JACK'S FAKE CASH
REGISTER,**

**THE BROKEN
NINTENDO,**

**MY ROCK
COLLECTION...**

22

and then, just as we jumped out of the way,

"Uuuuuuuuhhhhh!"

The whole Toy House came down!

"Timmberrrr!" Jack yelled, like they do on TV when a tree falls in a forest.

Cuh-RASH!!!

The curtains poofed from the breeze it made when it fell. Marbles rolled like crazy, bumping into soldiers and crayons. A football bounced out the door and my jack ball followed it, like a little friend.

"Awesome!" Jack shouted.

I stood still, frozen. I could hear my heart beat really hard, like a drum inside.

Then I remembered that somewhere between the crash of the tea set and the cash register, something had bonked me on the top of the head. (I'm not sure what, but maybe the crayon pot.) I remembered this because now it hurt like crazy.

I touched the spot, *really* carefully. It was all sore and swollen.

And it was wet.

Slowly, I brought my hand down and looked. It was bloody.

I stopped breathing for a minute. A few last Monopoly dollars floated down like snowflakes as I plopped to the floor.

Chapter 3

Before the last Monopoly dollar hit the floor, Mom was there. Her eyes went from Jack to the mess to me. She kneeled down beside me so fast, her skirt went *foof.* "Uh-oh, Cleo," she said, looking at the place on top of my head.

Foof, Mom left for one second and came back with a wet washcloth. It was the new

one with the lamb on it. It felt cool when she gently put it on my head. When she took it away, the poor lamb was all stained red, like it had been in Jack's animal war. That's when I really knew that this day had switched over from normal to not-so-normal. (I think not-so-normal is fine, by the way, unless there's blood. Then it's so not fine.)

I heard Dad's heavy shoes on the stairs. He didn't look at the mess when he came in, just zoomed right over to me. "It's going to be okay, Cleo. Yep, it is," he said.

I sort of hate it when parents say that. You know they're just trying to make you feel better. Which makes you think that the thing you need to feel better about is worse than you'd hoped it was.

But I liked it when Dad lifted me, like I was as light as the Appalachian. "Upsy-daisy," he said.

He settled me in the backseat of our green station wagon. "Easy does it, that's the way." Dad buckled me in.

Mom went to tell Mrs. Davis what to do about the other kids while we went to the doctor. She brought me a sweater and I remembered I wasn't dressed. For some reason this was the thing that finally made me cry.

"Don't worry, baby," Mom said. "The doctor's used to kids showing up in their pajamas when they have to get there in a hurry."

I was SO glad I was wearing my favorite nightgown, the pink one with the roses. But I still kept crying.

As the car pulled away, I saw Jack peeking out the window. I just KNEW he was feeling really bad. I was his twin, so I just knew.

Dad was driving a little faster than usual. He had that look on his face he gets when

he's reading the newspaper or fixing something that's broken.

I wanted to stop crying before we got to the doctor's office. I talked to the dolls on my fake cell phone to calm myself down. "You and the Appalachian need to take care of Anne today," I told Rapunzel. "Make sure to put some milk in her tea. And if you brush her hair, it makes her relax."

My tears slowed down.

Chapter 4

We have two doctors at the office where we go. Dr. Eisenberg is skinny and nice.

Dr. Seigal is funny and round. He always makes that joke about our last name: "Ah, here comes the not-so-Small family!"

Dr. Eisenberg

was on duty on Stitches Saturday. I was glad, because I wasn't in the mood for jokes.

"Well, if it isn't my old pal Cleo." Dr. Eisenberg's voice was all soft. His glasses were so thick in the glass part that you couldn't exactly tell what his eyes looked like. He smelled like he had just eaten a tuna sandwich.

"Uh-HUH," he said when he inspected me.

I almost was going to cry again, but I held my breath and the tears went away.

Dr. Eisenberg spoke quietly to Mom and Dad, but the word "stitches" kind of jumps

out no matter how softly you say it. It's that kind of word.

Back in the car, Mom sat with me, my head on her lap. "You've got a bad cut, honey. You'll need some stitches."

"Stitches?" My tears started to come back. "Will it hurt?" It felt like the tears were waiting to hear the answer.

"Probably not a lot," Dad said. "The doc says your head is tough stuff."

The tears decided to go away for now.

I only knew two people with stitches (besides, you know, pirates and soldiers). One was Michael, the kid at school who was always falling off swings and trees and things. The other one was Cecil, the mailman, who cut his hand on the carving knife at Thanksgiving. Even Jack hadn't had stitches yet.

I was getting stitches? It made me feel like a different kind of person than I thought I was.

Plus, it made me really nervous.

Chapter 5

We had to go to the big hospital, which I knew about because my mother went there to have babies. (She's had six, so she'd been there a lot.) On the way, Mom made up a little song, like she always does in tricky situations:

"A baseball player hits the ball,
No matter what the pitch is.

Let's hope the ball does not hit HIM,
Or he'll end up with stitches!"

We met a nurse who wore a striped outfit, like the peppermints in Candy Land.

"Well, aren't you the cutest little thing!" she said. "I just *love* your nightie!"

The Peppermint Nurse had really thick white shoes that squished when she walked. She was even a faster walker than my dad, who walks twice as fast as me, so I felt like we were sort of racing down the long hallways. Mom's skirt *foofed* around the corners as she tried to keep up.

Finally we stopped in a little white room

with big lights and a doctor I didn't know. He smiled at me in a way that made me let go of Dad and smile back.

"Well, what have we here? Hello, Miss Small. I'm Doctor Steve." He patted the bed. I lay down and the Peppermint Nurse pulled a sheet up under my chin. It was so white, it was like the Winter White crayon in September.

The doctor's hands felt all warm and heavy when he parted my hair. The nurse sprayed something cold on the cut.

"Okay, here we go. This shouldn't hurt much, but you just scream if it does," Dr. Steve said.

I held Mom's hand tight. I squeezed my eyes shut. The tears were back, waiting to see how much it hurt.

It didn't. Not a lot, anyway, just a little. Not like getting a shot. I breathed a big breath in and out.

While Dr. Steve stitched, I thought about the sewing kit Aunt Minnie gave me. I sewed a strawberry-shaped pincushion. I remembered the big needle going in and out of the polka-dot fabric.

Mom sang:

"I had a little friend who liked
To ride around with witches,

Till she fell off a broom one day,
And had to go get stitches!"

Dr. Steve laughed.

"I knew a little cowboy once
Who rode a horse, in britches,
Till one day that cute pony bucked!
The cowboy got some stitches!"

The Peppermint Nurse patted my arm. It was over.

"Okay, miss, good as new." Doctor Steve helped me sit up.

"Will I have a scar?"

"Oh, my, my, yes! Nine stitches? You'll have a beauty! But your hair will cover it: it'll be your little secret."

I was now officially a person with stitches! *Nine* of them! I was going to have a *scar*, like a pirate has, or Michael. (Well, he has about four of them.) I felt my tears go way away.

"Okay, princess, your carriage awaits."

Dad opened his arms to carry me back to the car.

"Ummmmmm, that's okay, Dad, I'll walk," I said. For once, he walked only medium-fast, so I kept up.

"When you go biking, wear a helmet,
Even if it itches!
Or else, if you fall off your bike,
Well, yikes! You might need stitches!"

47

Chapter 6

Coming home felt like when we come back from our summer vacation in the mountains. Everything seemed really familiar but kind of new at the same time.

I went upstairs right away to check on poor Anne and Rapunzel and the Appalachian. There they were, all confused, lying in a pile where I'd left them, next to the lamb washcloth.

"Awww, you've had a rough day. You need a little rest," I told the dolls. First I folded over the washcloth so we wouldn't have to see the bloody spot. Then I put them in my bed and pulled the sheet up under their chins, like the Peppermint Nurse would do.

The mess in my room looked smaller than I remembered, but it was still pretty big.

"Don't you worry, honey," Dad said. "Your brother and I will handle this."

Jack helped Dad put the Toy House back up. Nobody had ever really gotten mad at Jack for tipping it over because they were too busy taking me to get stitches. But he was quiet and did what he was told, which was not the usual Jack, trust me.

Jenna sorted the Monopoly pieces and then moved on to Candy Land. I picked up crayons. The Wild Blue Yonder was under the bed and I found Electric Lime in the hall. But Dad told me I should take it easy, so I got in bed with the dolls and just watched the mess disappear.

"I think we should have a party to celebrate Stitches Saturday," Mom said. "Cleo can wear the Princess Dress." That was my costume from last Halloween. I put on my tiara, too, but *very* carefully.

Mom put a cloth on the kitchen table and

mixed up some lemonade. She made pink frosting and spread it on graham crackers.

Jenna gave me a fan she'd gotten at our neighbor Emma's tenth birthday party. It was red with a Japanese house and some birds painted on it. "You can borrow this for today, since you got stitches. Just be gentle because it's made out of paper." (Jenna could be nice sometimes.)

Right about then Jack burst in the door. "Did you miss me?" He'd gone to Charles Variety to get me some lemon drops. (Plus a Mars bar that I could see peeking out of his pocket.)

Things were back to normal. The twins

were in their high chairs. Ray was exploring the pink frosting and Quinn was banging. "Yah, yah, yah!"

Lily sang a new little song while she licked her cracker.

"The cuckoo bird is cuckoo,
And I am cuckoo, too. Are youuuu . . . ?"

Mom made more frosting, blue this time, and Dad read the newspaper.

Me and Jack did the cannibal dance:

"WE are the CANnibals, bump bump,
WE are the CANnibals, bump bump . . ."

"Hey, come on, Jen," Jack called. It was definitely NOT normal for him to invite Jenna to join us, but it made her happy.

"Yeeeeaaaah, okay," she said and bumped Jack's butt with hers. "You should be careful bumping so you don't pop your stitches," she told me.

· · ·

That night, I let the dolls stay in bed with me.

"You were brave today, Cleo. Yes, you were," Dad said when he and Mom came in to say good night. "Just another Small disaster, hah!" Dad always says this when something bad happens in our family, after things are back to normal.

Dad lightly, *so* lightly, kissed the bandage on my head. "G'night and good dreams."

Mom hugged me for a long time, until I felt all warm and droopy.

She whispered:

"Your story's kinda gory,
But it has a moral, which is:
Beware a day that starts out normal.
It might end in stitches!"

Me and the dolls laughed.

After Mom and Dad went to bed, we talked for a while. I told them the whole story of the day, about the Peppermint Nurse and Dr. Eisenberg's thick glasses and everything.

"Whoa, what a day!" said Rapunzel. "What do you think will happen *tomorrow*?"

"Hmmmm . . ." I thought for a minute.

"Maybe I'll get a letter from the President of the United States!"

"Maybe you'll find a skunk in the back-yard," the Appalachian said. "Or a moose!"

"Or you'll get a new dress, a lacy pink one!" Anne whispered, all excited.

"Or maybe it'll just be a regular old day," I said, yawning.

"Probably," the dolls agreed. Then they were quiet and, one by one, they went to sleep.

Probably tomorrow *will* be just a normal day, I was thinking when my eyes closed. But after Stitches Saturday, I went to sleep not so sure.

3/10 ⑤